little hands
FLOWERS

Rachel Matthews

Chrysalis Children's Books

Flowers grow on plants and trees.
You can see flowers in parks, gardens and woodlands

Some even grow on plants in ponds.

Flowers grow in all sorts of shapes and sizes.

trumpet-shaped

ragged

saucer-shaped

spiky

bell-shaped

big

tiny

4

Some flowers have delicate petals.

Others have large, sturdy petals.

Flowering plants start life as a seed or a bulb.

You can plant a seed.

Keep the soil damp.
Watch what happens.

Buds have formed on this stem.
Inside the buds are the flowers.

This bud has
been cut in half.
Can you see
the petals?

When the buds open
the flowers bloom.

Look inside a flower.
The orange dust is
called pollen.

Flowers need pollen to produce new seeds.
Animals carry pollen from one flower to another.

How many colours can you see in this bunch of flowers?

Colourful petals attract insects and birds.
The patterns can show them where to find pollen.

Some flowers have a strong scent.

lavender

Other flowers
have no scent.

pansies

14

Smell some different flowers.
Which scent do you like best?

Some flowers use their scent to attract insects and birds.

We use scented
oils from flowers
to make perfume,
soap and shampoo.

When a plant has flowered, seeds are left behind.

Often the seeds are protected inside a fruit or pod. The tomatoes growing on this plant have seeds inside them.

We use flowers to decorate our homes and places of worship.

Have you ever worn or carried flowers at a special occasion?

Put some flowers between two pieces of paper with heavy books on top.

Make a picture with the dried flowers.

Notes for teachers and parents

Pages 2–3
Activity: Take the children for a walk around a garden or park to see a variety of flowering plants, including trees in blossom and plants such as water lilies growing on the surface of a pond.
Discussion: Compile a set of rules for appropriate behaviour, eg. looking at or taking photos of flowers rather than picking them, being aware of stinging insects such as bees and not dropping litter in the park. Talk about why each rule is important.

Pages 4–5
A flower's shape is often linked to the method of pollination – birds may use more robust petals as a perch while feeding.
Activity: Show the children a range of different-shaped flowers. Try counting the number of petals and make size comparisons.
Discussion: Talk about how each flower could be described, eg. "This flower is like a long, pointed spear."
Activity: Show the children examples of how artists such as Georgia O'Keeffe have tried to capture the shape and texture of flowers. Encourage the children to make paintings of their own.

Pages 6–9
Planting seeds allows children to explore the conditions necessary for germination.
Activity: Invite a keen gardener to talk to the children about growing plants from seed. Display examples of flowering plants.
Experiment: Set up parallel experiments by planting seeds in two pots. Water one pot and leave the other dry to show the children that water is necessary for germination.
Activity: Once seedlings have begun to appear, show the children the same plant at a later stage in its growth, when it is in bud. Cut open the bud to show the tightly-packed petals ready to emerge and unfold.

Pages 10–17
In plants that produce colourful, patterned or scented flowers, the flowers' main job is to attract pollinators such as bees, birds and butterflies. In wind-pollinated plants the flowers are unspectacular and unscented. Pollen is produced by the male parts of a flower and has to be transferred to the female parts before seeds can be produced.
Activity: Ask the children to describe the scent of some flowers.
Discussion: Tell the children that the world's largest plant, the rafflesia, produces a smell of rotten meat to attract flies. What do they think the chocolate cosmos smells of?
Activity: The children could dry some lavender flowers and use them to fill small fabric bags to give as gifts.

Pages 18–19
Link the growth of a fruit to a flowering plant's life cycle. Explain that the fruit is the part of a plant that contains seeds, so cucumbers, pea pods, avocadoes and the spiky cases surrounding horse chestnuts are all examples of fruits.
Activity: Cut open some fruits and count the number of seeds inside. Show the children the 'ripe' seed pod of a plant such as a petunia or love-in-a-mist (you could mention that the seed pod is the fruit of the plant because it contains seeds). The children could collect the seeds and make seed packets, 'labelling' them with pictures of the plants from which they were obtained.
Discussion: Explain to the children that they should never touch or eat the seeds of a plant unless an adult tells them it is safe to do so – the seeds of some plants are poisonous.

Pages 20–21
Discussion: Have the children seen flowers used as decoration? They may have seen, worn or carried flowers at a wedding. They may attend a place of worship that is decorated with flowers, particularly during festivals.

Page 22
Activity: Arrange flowers to be dried between sheets of blotting paper and leave pressed between heavy books for a couple of weeks. The children could make greetings cards with their dried flower pictures.

Index

First published in the UK in 2005 by
Chrysalis Children's Books
An imprint of Chrysalis Books Group Plc
The Chrysalis Building, Bramley Road
London W10 6SP

Copyright © Chrysalis Books Group Plc 2005

All rights reserved.

ISBN 1 84458 175 6

British Library Cataloguing in Publication Data for this book is available from the British Library.

Associate publisher Joyce Bentley
Project manager and editor Penny Worm
Art director Sarah Goodwin
Designer Patricia Hopkins
Picture researchers Veneta Bullen, Miguel Lamas
Photographer Ray Moller

The author and publishers would like to thank the following people for their contributions to this book: Ruth Thomson, Mary Conquest and Eliza Creedy-Smith.

Printed in China

10 9 8 7 6 5 4 3 2 1

Typography Natascha Frensch

Read Regular, READ SMALLCAPS and Read Space; European Community Design Registration 2003 and Copyright © Natascha Frensch 2001-2004 Read Medium, Read Black and Read Slanted Copyright © Natascha Frensch 2003-2004

READ™ is a revolutionary new typeface that will enhance children's understanding through clear, easily recognisable character shapes. With its evenly spaced and carefully designed characters, READ™ will help children at all stages to improve their literacy skills, and is ideal for young readers, reluctant readers and especially children with dyslexia.

Picture acknowledgements
All reasonable efforts have been made to ensure the reproduction of content has been done with the consent of copyright owner. If you are aware of any unintentional omissions please contact the publishers directly so that any necessary corrections may be made for future editions.
Corbis: Roy Morsch 16, Keren Su 20, Roy McMahon 21; Getty Images: Stuart Westmorland 3; Papilio: Ken Wilson 11.